Guinea Pigs
Don't Read Books

GUINEA PIGS DON'T READ BOOKS

Colleen Stanley Bare

PHOTOGRAPHS BY THE AUTHOR

A PUFFIN UNICORN

To Michelle

PUFFIN BOOKS
Published by the Penguin Group
Penguin Books USA Inc., 375 Hudson Street, New York, New York 10014, U.S.A.
Penguin Books Ltd, 27 Wrights Lane, London W8 5TZ, England
Penguin Books Australia Ltd, Ringwood, Victoria, Australia
Penguin Books Canada Ltd, 10 Alcorn Avenue, Toronto, Ontario, Canada M4V 3B2
Penguin Books (N.Z.) Ltd, 182–190 Wairau Road, Auckland 10, New Zealand

Penguin Books Ltd, Registered Offices: Harmondsworth, Middlesex, England

First published in the United States of America by Dodd, Mead and Company, 1985
Published by Scholastic Publications Ltd., 1986
Published by Puffin Books, 1993

1 3 5 7 9 10 8 6 4 2

Text copyright © Colleen Stanley Bare, 1985
Photographs copyright © Colleen Stanley Bare, 1985
All rights reserved
Library of Congress Catalog Card Number: 92-83708
ISBN 0-14-054995-1
Printed in Hong Kong

Unicorn® is a registered trademark of Dutton Children's Books

Guinea pigs don't read books, count numbers, run computers,

play checkers, or watch TV, but there are other things they do.

They chew, and chew, and chew.
Foods like apples, celery, carrots,

and if you don't
watch out,
they'll chew your
toys.

Guinea pigs see well
and stare at you.

They hear well
and listen.

They smell well
and sniff and sniff.

Guinea pigs make sounds.
They growl, grunt, gurgle,
purr, squeal, whistle,
and squeak,
squeak,
squeak.

Guinea pigs don't wear hats,
but they do wear fur coats.

Short, soft smooth ones

rough, bristly ones

long, silky ones.

Their coats come in many colors.

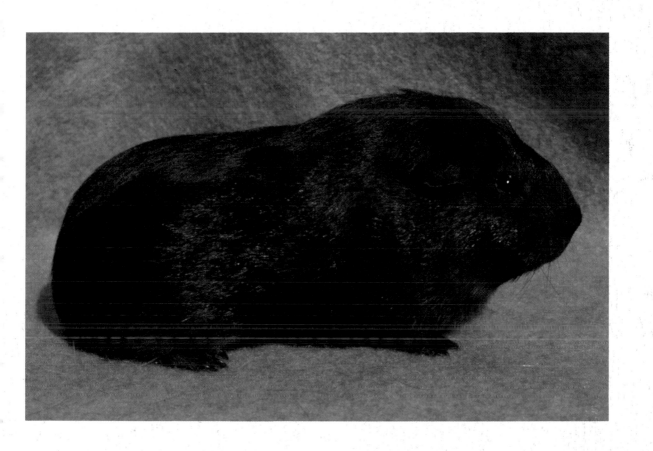

Blue, beige, cream,
red, orange, lilac,
chocolate, white, black.

And in mixtures of colors.

Guinea pigs aren't pigs.
They don't eat like pigs,
            walk like pigs,
            sound like pigs.
Even baby guinea pigs
don't look like baby pigs.

Guinea pigs like to be held
and hugged.
They are gentle
and calm
and lovable.

Guinea pigs may not
read books,
but they can be your
friends.